10/99

Palo Alto City Library

ABIGAIL TAKES THE WHEEL

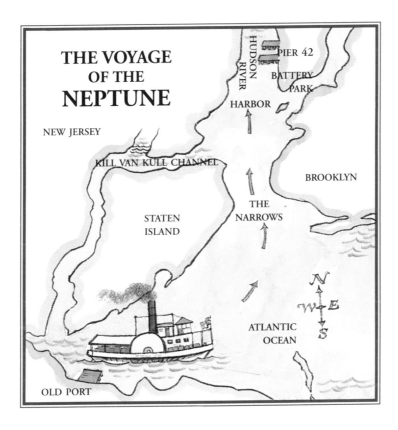

THE VOYAGE
OF THE
NEPTUNE

HUDSON RIVER

PIER 42

BATTERY PARK

HARBOR

NEW JERSEY

KILL VAN KULL CHANNEL

BROOKLYN

STATEN ISLAND

THE NARROWS

ATLANTIC OCEAN

N
W E
S

OLD PORT

An I Can Read Chapter Book™

ABIGAIL TAKES THE WHEEL

STORY BY Avi

PICTURES BY Don Bolognese

HarperCollins*Publishers*

For Ruby
—A.

To my daughter Annie
—D.B.

CONTENTS

Chapter 1 THE *NEPTUNE*

Abigail and her brother, Tom, watched as farmers loaded vegetables onto the freight boat *Neptune*. The *Neptune* was their home, and their father, Captain Bates, was the boat's captain. Every morning the boat took vegetables from Old Port, New Jersey, to New York City, twenty miles away. The *Neptune* took Abigail and Tom to school in New York City, too.

That morning, the first mate, Mr. Oliver, did not look very well.

"Are you all right, Mr. Oliver?" Abigail shouted down.

"My stomach is a bit upset," he called back. "I'll get over it."

"Morning, Abigail and Tom," Captain Bates said. "Ready for school?"

"I have a test today," Abigail said.

"Where's Ma?" Tom asked.

"She's going to stay in Old Port to visit Aunt Sally. She'll be waiting when we get back. Now, Abigail, don't fret," Captain Bates said. "We'll push off soon and be in the city by eight. Tom, get ready."

Tom climbed onto the front window ledge. From there he could pull the ship's whistle cord. His father let him pull it when they sailed. Abigail often got to steer the boat while her father stood nearby. They called her "First Mate Abigail," and everybody said she was a good sailor.

Mr. Oliver came to the pilot house. "Everything is loaded, Captain," he said.

"How are you feeling?" Captain Bates asked him.

"Not great," the first mate said. "But I can manage."

"Time to go, Tom!" Captain Bates called. "Pull the whistle cord." A long blast sounded.

"Start the engines," Captain Bates shouted into the speaking tube. The tube ran down below to the engine room, where the engineer worked. "Set the wheels turning at four strokes per minute. We need to get these kids to school!"

Mr. Oliver cast off the ropes. Smoke poured from the stack. The side paddles began to churn. The *Neptune* eased from the dock. Abigail and Tom were going to school.

Chapter 2   IN THE NARROWS

As the *Neptune* entered the Narrows, choppy waves made the boat rock.

"The main channel is crowded this morning," the captain said. "With the breeze coming down, it might be a bit rough. Tom, be ready with the whistle."

There were ships everywhere. Some were going toward New York City. Just as many were leaving.

Suddenly Captain Bates called, "Look there! Doesn't that ship know the harbor rules? This isn't Sunday sailing! Look out! Those ships are going to crash!"

A large sailing ship, the *Bonnie Brea*, had been entering the harbor. Right in front of her was the *Pelham*. Each one tried to turn away. But the wind and tide were too strong. With a crash, the two ships struck.

The *Pelham* lost its topsail but was able to sail on. The *Bonnie Brea* lost its forward sails and could not sail. She began to drift.

"I think we'd better offer to help,"
the captain said. He guided the *Neptune*
toward the drifting ship.

"Do you need a hand?" he called to
the men on the *Bonnie Brea*.

"Can you tow us to the city?" they called. "We'll pay you well!"

"Be glad to!" Captain Bates said. He turned toward the speaking tube. "The *Bonnie Brea* needs a tow. Harbor laws say if we tow her I have to handle her wheel. As soon as Mr. Oliver helps tie up the tow rope, he'll pilot us to the city."

"Yes, sir!" replied the engineer.

"Abigail, can you steer us alongside that ship?" the captain asked.

"I think so," Abigail said.

"Tom, help Abigail until Mr. Oliver gets here." The captain left the pilot house.

Abigail called into the speaking tube, "Three strokes, then a stop."

The engineer's voice said, "All right, First Mate Abigail."

bow

stern

BRE

UNI

Chapter 3 ABIGAIL AT THE WHEEL

Abigail guided the *Neptune* alongside the *Bonnie Brea*. Captain Bates climbed aboard. A long, heavy rope was dropped from the sailing ship's bow. Mr. Oliver tied it fast to the *Neptune*'s stern.

"They're ready," Tom told his sister.

"We need to go slow and steady," said Abigail. She pulled the speaking tube toward her. "Forward two strokes," she said,

The *Neptune*'s side wheels turned. She began to go upstream. "Give one pull to the whistle cord," Abigail said. "That will tell everybody we're going straight on."

Tom pulled the cord.

The *Neptune* moved forward. The tow rope stretched tight and the *Bonnie Brea* was pulled along. The strain of the towing and the choppy water made the freight boat rock from side to side.

Abigail held the large wheel with both hands. "It's awfully rough," she said. "I hope I'm strong enough to handle this."

"Don't worry," Tom said. "You won't have to do it for long."

Mr. Oliver came in. He looked sick.

"What's the matter?" Tom asked.

"I feel worse," Mr. Oliver said as he took the wheel.

"Do you want help?" Abigail asked.

"I think I'm okay." He sounded unsure.

"Are we going to be late for school?" Tom asked.

"A little, maybe," Mr. Oliver said. "But a towing job brings a lot of money. Besides, they want to go to Pier Forty-two."

"That's close to our school," Abigail said.

"We'll get . . . there," Mr. Oliver said. He was looking worse and worse.

Suddenly he said, "Abigail, you'd better take over. I'm really sick." With a groan he staggered out of the pilot house.

Abigail grabbed the wheel again.

"What do we do now?" Tom asked.

"How many times have we gone to New York?" Abigail asked.

"A million, maybe," Tom said.

"Then we must know the way," Abigail said. She gripped the wheel tightly. "I need to keep both hands on the wheel. Swing the speaking tube toward you, Tom. Tell the engineer we need more power."

"Three strokes forward," Tom shouted.

"Is that you, Tom?" the engineer asked. "Where's Mr. Oliver?"

"He got sick," Tom said. "Abigail is at the wheel again."

"Abigail," shouted the engineer, "can you handle it?"

Abigail called back, "I think so!"

Chapter 4 Up the Hudson River

Abigail steered the *Neptune* to the Kill Van Kull channel, then turned the boat. Now they were heading right for New York City.

"How's the *Bonnie Brea* doing?" Abigail asked.

"Pretty good," Tom said.

A Staten Island ferry came toward the *Neptune*. It blew two blasts of its whistle.

That meant it wished to pass on the right.

"Tom, tell the ferry we understand," Abigail said.

Tom pulled the whistle cord twice.

Abigail steered the *Neptune* to the left. The ferry passed to the right. The *Neptune* swept by Battery Park and up the Hudson River.

Suddenly a huge ship, the *Bristol*, appeared. She was moving right across the *Neptune*'s bow.

"That ship shouldn't be there!" Tom said.

"I know," Abigail said. "Pull the whistle cord once. We need to pass her." The *Neptune*'s whistle sounded.

The *Bristol* returned two angry blasts.

"She won't let you go by!" Tom shouted.

"Doesn't she know the harbor rules?"

Abigail looked forward and back. There was not enough room for her and the *Bonnie Brea* to pass. If she did not stop, the *Neptune* would be struck by the *Bristol*.

"Pull the cord four times," she cried. "We must stop!"

Tom made the whistle shriek and shouted into the tube, "Stop engines!"

The paddle wheels stopped. But it is hard to stop a boat when it's moving in water. The *Neptune* continued to go forward.

Abigail cried, "Reverse engines!"

The paddles churned backward. First the *Neptune* stopped its forward motion. Then it began to move backward.

The *Bristol* swept past the *Neptune*.

Abigail looked behind. The *Bonnie Brea* had not stopped. It was drawing close, much too close.

"She's going to hit us!" Tom said.

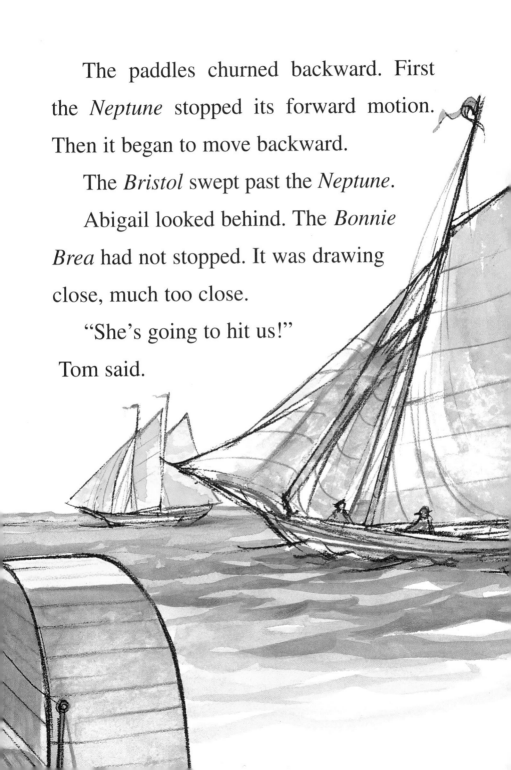

"Stop engines!" Abigail cried.

"Stop engines," Tom shouted in the tube.

The paddle wheels stopped turning.

"Forward engines!" Abigail now cried. "Fast!"

"Four strokes forward!" Tom called.

The *Neptune* lurched forward.

Abigail struggled to turn the wheel.

The *Neptune* swung about, away from the *Bonnie Brea*. The tow rope pulled tight.

"Hurrah!" Tom shouted. "The *Bonnie Brea*'s right again."

Abigail sighed with relief.

They continued up the river.

"I see Pier Forty-two!" Tom said.

Pier Forty-two was shaped like a gigantic letter U. It looked easy to get into.

Then Abigail's heart jumped. A large holiday boat, the *Peekskill*, was pulling out of Pier Forty-two. It was coming right at them.

Chapter 5   PIER FORTY-TWO

"Look out!" Tom called. He pulled the whistle cord. A warning blast sounded.

Abigail knew the whistle was not enough. Unless she turned the *Neptune* away from the pier and into the middle of the river, the *Peekskill* and the *Neptune* would collide. She pulled the wheel so hard, her feet lifted off the deck.

The *Peekskill* heard and saw the *Neptune*. Its wheels turned faster and faster. It moved away from the *Neptune*.

"The pier is empty," Tom hollered.

"But now we're going away from Pier Forty-two!" Abigail cried. "We'll have to make almost a complete circle to get back. Keep watching! I have to make sure the *Bonnie Brea* doesn't run into us."

Abigail swung the wheel around. The *Neptune* began to circle back to the pier.

"Tom," Abigail warned, "if I stop, the *Bonnie Brea* will hit us. Keep that whistle blowing! Make sure every ship knows what we're doing!"

The whistle shrieked and shrieked.

The men on the pier saw the *Neptune*
approach with the sailing ship in tow.
Frantically they worked to fling rope
bumpers over the wooden pier piles, to keep
the sailing ship from smashing into the pier.

Now both boats—the *Neptune* first, the *Bonnie Brea* behind—were between the arms of the pier.

"We're almost there!" Tom cried.

Abigail gripped the wheel tightly and aimed the *Neptune* right for the head of the pier. Closer and closer they came. Just when it looked as if the *Neptune* was going to crash, Abigail hauled the wheel down and around.

The *Neptune* made a tight turn inside the pier's arms and began to head out toward the river. The *Bonnie Brea* kept coming in. The *Neptune* passed her with just a few feet to spare. The sailing ship nosed into the top of the pier. When she hit the bumpers, she stopped.

"Stop engines!" Abigail cried.

The *Neptune*'s engines stopped. The freight boat nestled against the pier.

Abigail leaned against the wheel. She had never been so tired in her life.

Tom hugged her. "You did it!"

"Abigail!" said another voice. It was her father. He had hurried onto the *Neptune*. "Where's Mr. Oliver?" he asked.

"He got sick and went below," Tom said.

Captain Bates was astonished. "But . . . Abigail, was that you at the wheel?"

She nodded.

"Abigail," he said, "you are amazing!"

"What time is it?" she asked.

Captain Bates checked his pocket watch. "Almost eight."

"School!" Abigail cried. "My test!"

"Hurry!" Tom shouted.

The two children ran off the ship and into the busy New York City streets.

Chapter 6 CAPTAIN ABIGAIL

At three-thirty Abigail and Tom finished school and started back to the *Neptune*.

As soon as they saw the *Neptune*, its whistle gave a long shriek.

"I guess Dad wants us to hurry," Abigail said.

The two children ran to the gangplank, where their father was waiting. Next to him

was Mr. Oliver, looking much better. The *Neptune*'s engineer was also there. So, too, was the crew from the *Bonnie Brea*.

"Attention!" Captain Bates cried.

All the men stood stiffly.

"Welcome aboard," Captain Bates called to his children. "The crews of the *Neptune* and the *Bonnie Brea* await you."

As Abigail and Tom walked up the gangplank, all the men saluted.

"Tom," his father said, "you are hereby appointed First Mate."

He turned to his daughter and shook her hand. "Abigail, from this day forward, you also have a new rank: Captain Abigail!"

"Hurrah for First Mate Tom!" the men shouted. Then even louder they cried, "Hurrah for Captain Abigail!"

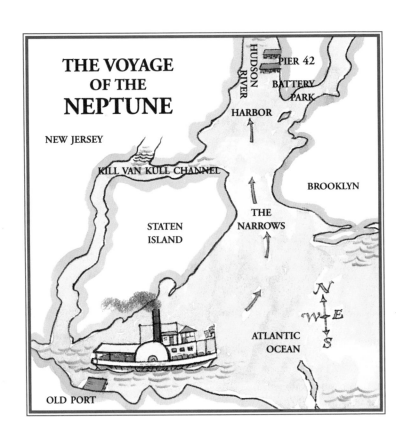

THE VOYAGE
OF THE
NEPTUNE

HUDSON RIVER

PIER 42

BATTERY PARK

HARBOR

NEW JERSEY

KILL VAN KULL CHANNEL

BROOKLYN

THE NARROWS

STATEN ISLAND

ATLANTIC OCEAN

OLD PORT

N
W E
S

AUTHOR'S NOTE

In the 1880s, the port of New York was one of the busiest in the United States, and indeed the world. There was a great deal of shipping commerce, both national and international, as well as many boats carrying travelers and immigrants. Much of the local shipping brought goods to the City of New York from upper New York State, Long Island, and New Jersey. At the time, New Jersey was one of the city's principal suppliers of vegetables and fruits—hence its nickname, "The Garden State."

This was a period of transition in the design of boats. Though there was a great variety of steam-driven ships, sailing ships still plied the waves, both for coastal destinations and for crossing oceans.

Abigail Takes the Wheel is based on a story published in 1881 in the children's magazine *St. Nicholas*. The tale was presented as neither fiction nor nonfiction, simply as an account of something heroic that happened in New York City's busy port. My own guess is that the story is true.

HarperCollins®, ☎®, and I Can Read Book® are trademarks of HarperCollins Publishers Inc.

Abigail Takes the Wheel
Text copyright © 1999 by Avi
Illustrations copyright © 1999 by Don Bolognese
Printed in the U.S.A. All rights reserved.

Library of Congress Cataloging-in-Publication Data
Avi, date
   Abigail takes the wheel / story by Avi ; pictures by Don Bolognese.
      p.   cm.
   "An I can read Chapter book."
   Summary: When the first mate of the freight boat Neptune falls ill, it is up to Abigail, the captain's daughter, to
steer the ship up the Hudson River from New Jersey to New York City.
   ISBN 0-06-027662-2. — ISBN 0-06-027663-0 (lib. bdg.)
   [1. Cargo ships—Fiction.   2. Ships—Fiction.   3. Fathers and daughters—Fiction.
4. New York (N.Y.)—Fiction.   I. Bolognese, Don, ill.   II. Title.
PZ7.A953Ab   1999   98-3688
[Fic]—dc21   CI
                                                                                              A

                        1   2   3   4   5   6   7   8   9   10
                                          ❖
                                  First Edition